Dirty Bertie

FETCH!

For Julia, Edward and Mickey-Love

~ D R

For Zoe, Ed, Arthur, Maisie and Tess the dog

~ A M

STRIPES PUBLISHING
An imprint of Magi Publications
I The Coda Centre, 189 Munster Road,
London SW6 6AW

A paperback original
First published in Great Britain in 2010

Characters created by David Roberts
Text copyright © Alan MacDonald, 2010
Illustrations copyright © David Roberts, 2010

ISBN: 978-1-84715-124-7

Dirty Bertie

FETCH!

DAVID ROBERTS WRITTEN BY ALAN MACDONALD

Stripes

Collect all the
Dirty Bertie books!

Contents

FETCH!

CHAPTER 1

DING DONG.

"Bertie, can you get that?" called Mum.
Bertie scooted into the hall and opened
the front door.

"Special delivery!" said the postman,
handing him a brown parcel.

It was addressed to Master Bertie
Burns. Wait a minute – that was him!

"I GOT A
PRESENT!
I GOT A
PRESENT!" he yelled,
bursting into the kitchen.

"It's not fair!" grumbled Suzy.
"Why didn't *I* get anything?"

"Cos no one likes you," said Bertie,
sticking out his tongue.

Mum was looking at the postmark.
"It must be a late birthday present.
I think it's from Uncle Ed in America."

Bertie gasped. Rich Uncle Ed? He sent
the coolest presents – even if they never
arrived on time.

Bertie tore off the
wrapping paper.
He stared. It *wasn't*!
It *couldn't* be!

Dirty Bertie

"Ha ha! It's a toy dog," said Suzy.

"No it isn't, it's a ROBODOG!"
whooped Bertie.

He read the label tied round the collar.

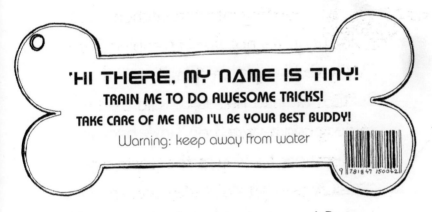

'HI THERE, MY NAME IS TINY!
TRAIN ME TO DO AWESOME TRICKS!
TAKE CARE OF ME AND I'LL BE YOUR BEST BUDDY!
Warning: keep away from water

This was the best present ever! Better
even than the prehistoric dino-poop
Darren had given him for his birthday.
Think of all the things he could do with
a robot! Tiny could keep intruders out of
Bertie's bedroom. He'd train him to bark
at Miss Boot and to bite Know-All Nick.
Wait till his friends heard about this –

he'd be the envy of the whole school!

Whiffer trotted over and sniffed Tiny suspiciously. What kind of dog was this? It didn't even *smell* like a dog!

Suzy folded her arms. "So what does it do then?"

"I have to train him first," replied Bertie, reading the instructions.

He found a switch on Tiny's back and flicked it on.

CLICK! WHIRR, WHIRR!

Tiny stirred into life. His eyes flashed red and his head wagged from side to side. Bertie set him on the ground and grabbed the remote control. He pressed a button.

"Sit, Tiny!" he commanded.

BEEP, BEEP! CLICK, CLICK!

Tiny folded his back legs and sat down.

Dirty Bertie

"Amazing!" gasped Dad.

"Wonderful!" said Mum.

Whiffer looked puzzled. No one ever got this excited when *he* sat down.

"Lie down, Tiny!" said Bertie.

WHIRR, CLICK! Tiny lay down.

Now for the big one, thought Bertie.

Dirty Bertie

"Come, Tiny!" he said, patting his knees. "Come to me!"

CLICK, WHIRR! BEEP, BEEP!

Tiny's little legs began to move and he plodded jerkily across the floor.

"Look! He's doing it – he's walking!" cried Bertie.

"Oh, isn't that sweet?" said Mum.

Whiffer growled. He'd seen quite enough. It was time to put this imposter in his place.

GRRR!

He pounced, pinning Tiny to the floor.

Dirty Bertie

BEEP! WHIRR!

GRRR!

"NO, WHIFFER! BAD BOY!" yelled Bertie, grabbing him by the collar and yanking him off.

Whiffer hung his head. What had he done now?

Bertie opened the back door and shoved him towards it. "OUT!"

WHAM! The door slammed shut.

Whiffer padded to the window and watched everyone crowd round the new dog, smiling and clapping. His ears drooped. What was going on? One moment he was Bertie's best friend, the next he'd been replaced by a flat-faced mutt who walked like a puppet. Well, he wasn't taking this lying down. He'd show that pesky pooch who was top dog!

CHAPTER 2

Next morning, Whiffer lay in wait for the postman. Before long a pile of letters thudded on to the mat.

WOOF! WOOF! He bounded into the hall excitedly.

WHIRR, WHIRR! BEEP, BEEP!

Too late – Tiny had got there first. He scooped up the letters in his mouth and trundled past with red eyes flashing. Whiffer drooped after him into the kitchen.

Tiny stopped beside Dad and wagged his tail.

BEEP! RUFF! RUFF!

Dad looked down. "Well, look at this! Tiny's brought the post! Who's a clever boy?"

He patted the little robot on the head and took the letters.

"I've been training him," said Bertie, proudly. "Roll over, Tiny."

Tiny rolled over.

"I must say he's very well behaved." Mum smiled. "Not like *some* dogs I could mention."

"He does everything I tell him," said Bertie. "Watch this!"

He pressed a green button on the remote control. "Dance, Tiny!"

WHIRR, CLICK! ZOOB, ZIB!

Tinny music blared out and Tiny rocked from side to side performing a cute little dance.

"Oh, that's soooo sweet!" cooed Suzy.

Dad looked up from his letter. "Yes and what's more, he doesn't leave hairs on the sofa."

"Or go crazy when the doorbell goes," said Mum.

"And he won't poo on Mrs Nicely's lawn," said Suzy.

They all turned to look at Whiffer.

WOOF! barked Whiffer. *Finally* someone was paying him some attention! His bowl was empty and he was starving. He picked it up and

Dirty Bertie

dropped it at Dad's feet. Dad went on
reading his letter. Whiffer padded over to
Mum. But she was busy talking to Suzy.

What was the matter with everyone?
He carried his bowl over to Bertie and
plonked it down.

WOOF! he barked, gazing up at
Bertie with big, sad eyes. That usually
did the trick.

Dirty Bertie

"Not now, Whiffer, I'm busy!" sighed Bertie, fiddling with the remote.

Whiffer stared. What was going on? His bowl was empty! Wasn't anyone going to notice?

After lunch, Darren and Eugene came round to play. Bertie had told them all about Tiny. He took them out into the garden to show off some of Tiny's tricks. Whiffer trailed after them, hoping to play "Fetch" or "Chew the Slipper". Usually Darren made a fuss of him, but today he didn't seem to notice he was there.

"A real robot!" gasped Darren. "You lucky thing!"

"You could teach him to bring you breakfast in bed," said Eugene.

"And do your homework."

Mmm, it was a tempting idea, thought Bertie. But the instruction booklet only listed Ten Top Tricks like "Sit", "Fetch" and "Beg". All the same, that was ten more tricks than Whiffer could do. Whiffer was about as obedient as a lemon meringue. The thing about Tiny was you could take him anywhere. He didn't bark, he didn't whine and he didn't run off chasing squirrels. And best of all, Bertie was the only one of his friends who had a Robodog.

"Show us a trick," said Darren.

"Okay," said Bertie. "Tiny, lie down!"

WHIRR! CLICK! CLICK!

Tiny lay down.

"Good boy!" said Bertie. "Tiny, roll over!"

Tiny rolled over.

"Show me how you beg!"

Tiny sat up and raised both paws. His ears flopped pathetically.

"Wicked!" laughed Darren.

"Brilliant!" cried Eugene.

Whiffer watched in disbelief. This was too much!

WOOF! WOOF! He bounded over and began chasing his tail in circles.

"What's up with him?" asked Darren.

Dirty Bertie

Bertie shrugged. "Dunno. He's been acting weird ever since I got Tiny."

Tiny showed them how he could play dead. He did his little dance. He plodded over to a tree and cocked his leg. Darren and Eugene laughed as if it was the funniest thing they'd ever seen. Whiffer stared. This was so unfair! When *he* weed against the gate he got in big trouble!

"And wait till you see this," said Bertie, picking up a stick.

"Fetch, Tiny!" He threw the stick over Tiny's head. Whiffer saw his chance. He might not be able to dance, but no one was faster at fetching sticks. He leaped past Bertie, bounding after the stick.

WOOF! WOOF!

WOO—

Dirty Bertie

Hey! Someone had him by the collar!

"NO, WHIFFER. Leave it!" shouted
Bertie.

WHIRR! BEEP! CLICK, CLICK!

Tiny trundled over and picked up the
stick in his mouth. He brought it back to
Bertie and dropped it at his feet. Bertie
patted his head.

"Clever boy! Who's a good boy?"

Whiffer growled. *GRRR!* Call that a
stick? He'd show that stuck-up pup how
to fetch. He looked around. Ah ha! What
about that giant stick propping up the
washing line?

He bounded across the lawn and
seized the clothes prop in his mouth.

TWANG! The washing line sagged to
the ground, dragging Mum's sheets in
the mud.

Just at that moment, Mum stuck her
head out of the back door.

"Bertie, have you seen my ... ARGHH!
Look at my washing! It's filthy!"

"It wasn't me!" said Bertie. "It was
Whiffer!"

Whiffer tottered over, carrying the
giant pole in his mouth. He dropped it at
Mum's feet and wagged his tail, looking
pleased with himself.

Mum glared at him. "Bad Boy!
Get inside!"

CHAPTER 3

Over the next week, Whiffer's behaviour
only got worse. On Tuesday he left a
puddle on the landing. On Wednesday
he hid a filthy bone in Mum and Dad's
bed. On Thursday he tried to bury Tiny's
remote control in the garden. By Friday
Mum and Dad had had enough. They sat
Bertie down for a serious talk.

Dirty Bertie

"This has got to stop," said Mum.

"It can't go on," sighed Dad.

Bertie looked blank. What were they talking about? He hadn't kept worms in his room for ages – at least not anywhere they'd be found.

"What have I done now?" he asked.

"It's not you, it's Whiffer!" said Dad. "He's driving us crazy!"

"He keeps bringing sticks and bones into the house!" said Mum.

"He weed on the carpet!"

"He follows us everywhere!"

"It's not my fault!" grumbled Bertie.

"He's *your* dog," said Dad. "You're supposed to look after him."

"I do!"

"You don't!" said Mum. "Not since you got Tiny. Who took Whiffer to the park this week? Who fed him? Who cleared up his mess?"

Bertie stared at his feet. Perhaps he had neglected Whiffer a bit, but that was because he had so much to do. Tiny was just a puppy and he still needed training. Besides, it was so much fun.

Mum folded her arms. "I'm sorry, Bertie, but this isn't working. Whiffer's *jealous.*"

"JEALOUS?" said Bertie.

"Yes! He doesn't like having another dog around. And you ignoring him only makes it worse!"

"I WON'T ignore him," said Bertie. "I'll look after them both!"

Mum looked at Dad. "All right," she sighed. "We'll give it one more week."

"But Whiffer's got to stop driving us mad," said Dad.

CHAPTER 4

"Whiffer, walkies!"

WOOF! WOOF!

Whiffer flew out of the kitchen and pinned Bertie to the wall. It was ages since they'd gone for walkies. Walkies meant the park and the park meant squirrels.

"Good boy," said Bertie, clipping on his lead. "Tiny's coming too."

Dirty Bertie

Whiffer growled and showed his teeth.
GRRR! Not that mangy little mongrel!

Bertie opened the front door and
Whiffer took off, dragging him down the
path. Tiny wobbled along behind, beeping
and whirring. *This is great*, thought Bertie.
Me and my dogs, all friends together.

Dirty Bertie

The park was full of people walking their dogs. There were tall boxers, yappy terriers and fluffy poodles. But nobody else had a dog like Tiny. The other children crowded around Bertie enviously.

"Wow! Is he yours?" asked a little curly-haired girl.

"Yes," said Bertie. "He's called Tiny.

Dirty Bertie

Want to see him dance?"

Bertie made Tiny perform every one of his tricks. The crowd gasped and clapped. Whiffer looked away, bored.

"Can he fetch my ball?" asked the little girl.

"He can fetch anything," said Bertie, taking the rubber ball. He sent the ball bouncing across the grass.

"Fetch, Tiny!"

Dirty Bertie

CLICK, CLICK! WHIRR! Tiny set off.
But Whiffer had seen the ball too.
In a blur of speed, he overtook the
robot. Seconds later, he was back,
dropping the ball at Bertie's feet and
wagging his tail.

"No!" said Bertie. "Whiffer, stay. Let
Tiny get this one."

Bertie threw the ball as far as he
could. Whiffer forgot all about "Stay" –
he was much better at "Fetch". He set
off, racing past Tiny to get there first.
The ball bounced towards the pond.

DOINK! DOINK! … PLOP!

"TINY, NO, COME BACK…!" yelled
Bertie.

Too late. Whiffer plunged into the
water, scattering ducks in all directions.
Tiny followed, beetling along behind.

Dirty Bertie

Dirty Bertie

SPLASH!

WHIRR, WHIRR! ... BEEP! ... BLUB BLUB ... BLOOP!

Bubbles rose to the surface.

"TINY!" called Bertie. "TINY?"

Silence.

"He can't swim," said the little girl.

Bertie stared.

A moment later Whiffer arrived like a hurricane on four legs and flattened him on the grass. He was muddy, dripping wet and clutching a rubber ball. He dropped it on the grass and barked excitedly.

WOOF! WOOF!

"No! Ha ha! Get off!" giggled Bertie, as Whiffer licked his face.

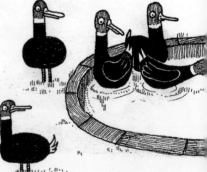

Dirty Bertie

He got up and ruffled Whiffer's fur.
"Good boy," he said. "Tell you what, let's
see if there's any squirrels."

WOOF! Whiffer took off like a furry
bolt of lightning. Bertie ran to catch up.
Tiny had been okay – for a robot – but
there really wasn't anyone like good
old Whiffer!

CHAPTER 1

Bertie opened the front door.

Gran zoomed past him and burst into the kitchen where Mum, Dad and Suzy were having tea. Bertie had never seen her so excited. She looked like she might take off.

"You'll never guess what!" she panted. "I'm going to meet the Queen!"

Dirty Bertie

"No!" gasped Mum.

"Yes!"

"Never!"

"I am. Look – here's the invitation!"

She fished in her handbag and pulled out a silver-trimmed card with an important-looking coat of arms.

Bertie, Suzy, Mum and Dad crowded round to look.

Her Majesty The Queen Graciously Invites

Mrs D. Burns and guest

To a *Royal Garden Party* at BUCKINGHAM PALACE
Saturday 3rd June

(Please Dress Posh)

Dirty Bertie

"Goodness! A royal garden party?" said Mum.

"Isn't it exciting?" said Gran. "I can hardly wait!"

Suzy read the invitation again.

"And guest," she said. "What does that mean?"

"It means I can bring a friend or relative," explained Gran.

"What? To meet the Queen?" asked Bertie, wide-eyed.

"Yes!"

"Actually really MEET her?"

"Yes, actually really."

Bertie could hardly believe his ears. Imagine that – going to a party at the Queen's house! Bertie loved parties and this would be the greatest ever. Think of the food – royal jelly and king-sized

ice creams. Think of the games – Musical
Thrones, Pass the Diamonds and Hide
and Seek with a hundred rooms to
choose from. Maybe the Queen would
decide to knight him? Maybe she'd even

let him borrow her
crown for a day to
wear to school? Hang
on though, didn't Gran
say she could only
take *one* guest to the
party? And she hadn't
said who it would be!

"Let me take your coat, Dotty," said
Mum, steering Gran into a chair.

"Are you comfy? I'll get you a
cushion!" simpered Suzy.

"Have some cake!" offered Dad,
cutting a huge slice of sponge.

Bertie scowled. He could see what his
sneaky family were up to. They wanted
Gran to choose them!

"Well? Have you decided?" asked
Mum.

"Decided what?"

"Who you're taking to the garden
party?"

"Oh yes," said Gran. She dabbed her lips with a napkin. "Well, it wasn't easy, I've got so many friends. But in the end I thought – who do I know that's never been to London? Who's never even seen Buckingham Palace?"

"ME!" yelled Bertie, banging into the table and spilling the cups.

"BERTIE?" gasped Suzy.

"Is that a good idea?" said Dad. "I mean Bertie – meeting the Queen?"

"Why shouldn't I meet her?" demanded Bertie.

"Well, it's just … sometimes you forget your manners."

"I don't!" said Bertie, grabbing another slice of cake.

Of course there was the time the lady Mayoress visited his school. That was a

bit of a disaster. But it wasn't easy to
shake hands with a bogey stuck to your
finger. Still, Bertie was sure he wouldn't
make the same mistake with the Queen.
She probably had servants to deal with
that sort of thing.

CHAPTER 2

Bertie couldn't wait to tell his friends at school. They were going to be so jealous! He waited until break time when they were out in the playground.

"What are you doing next Saturday?" he said.

Darren shrugged. "Nothing."

"I've got swimming," said Donna.

Dirty Bertie

"I've got to visit my aunt," said Eugene, gloomily.

"Oh. Only I won't be here," said Bertie. "I've got to go to London. To meet the Queen."

The others stared at him boggle-eyed. Darren burst out laughing.

"YOU? MEET THE QUEEN? HA HA!"

"Good one, Bertie," grinned Eugene. "For a minute I almost believed you."

"It's *true!*" said Bertie. "She's giving a gardening party. Me and Gran are invited."

"Invited to what?" asked a drawling voice. Bertie groaned. Trust Know-All Nick to poke his nose in where it wasn't wanted!

"Bertie reckons he's going to meet the Queen," grinned Darren.

Dirty Bertie

"Oh ha ha, very funny," sneered Nick.

"I am!" said Bertie.

"Liar liar, pants on fire!"

"All right, don't believe me," said Bertie, huffily.

"I don't," said Nick.

"Okay, I'll bring you the invitation."

Dirty Bertie

"Huh! Anyone could write an invitation," scoffed Nick. "Prove you met the Queen, then I might believe you."

"Right, I will!" said Bertie. "I'll get her photo. We'll soon see who's lying!"

The week went by slowly. As the big day drew near, Bertie's parents gave him lots of helpful advice.

"Don't mumble!" said Dad.

"Don't slouch!" said Mum.

"And please, please, please DON'T PICK YOUR NOSE!"

"I'm not going to," sighed Bertie. Anyone would think he had no manners at all!

Mum pulled up a chair. "All right, let's have a practice. Pretend I'm the Queen

Dirty Bertie

and we've just met. Now, what do
you say?"

"Um… Where's the food?" said
Bertie.

"You can't ask the Queen that!"

"Why not? I'll be hungry."

"You have to make Polite
Conversation," said Mum. "And
remember to call her 'Your
Majesty'. Now try again.
Ahem… Good afternoon,
young man."

"Good hafternoon, Your
Magicsty," said Bertie.

Dirty Bertie

Mum gave him a look. "Why are you talking like that?"

"I'm makin' polite what-you-said."

"You sound like you've got a mouthful of chewing gum. Speak normally! And stop bobbing up and down!"

"I'm bowing!" said Bertie.

"Well don't! Keep still and talk to me. And hurry up, the Queen hasn't got all day!"

"Good afternoon, Your Magicsty," said Bertie. "Um, when do we eat?"

Mum gave up. There would be hundreds of people at the garden party. With any luck, Bertie wouldn't get within a mile of the Queen. She certainly hoped not.

CHAPTER 3

The great day finally dawned. At ten o'clock on Saturday morning, Bertie knocked on Gran's front door. Gran did a double take. Was this really her grandson? Bertie's face shone, his hair was neatly parted and he was wearing a tie.

"My goodness!" she cried. "I hardly

recognized you. You look as if you've been polished!"

Gran took his picture. Then Bertie took a picture of Gran in her new dress and hat. Then they set off for the station.

Just after two o'clock they presented themselves at the palace gates. A man wearing a smart uniform showed them through to the biggest garden Bertie had ever seen. It had wide green lawns, magnificent fountains and statues with bare bottoms. Across the lawn, hundreds of people were spilling out of an enormous white tent.

Bertie stared. How was he going to meet the Queen with all this lot?

Inside the tent, things didn't get any better. He could hardly move without treading on someone's foot or being poked by a handbag. Bertie sighed. Where was the party food? The royal jelly and ice cream? A waiter passed by with a tray of dainty cucumber sandwiches. Bertie took one and crammed it into his mouth. It would hardly have fed a goldfish.

He looked around. This was going to be the worst party ever. Everyone was nearly as old as Gran – and all they did was stand around talking and sipping tea. Worst of all, the Queen hadn't even bothered to turn up! Bertie had been keeping an eye out for someone wearing a sparkly gold crown, but there was no sign of her. At this rate he would never get a photo. What would he tell all his friends?

Dirty Bertie

Dirty Bertie

"BERTIE!" hissed Gran.

"What?"

"Don't eat so fast. And don't say 'what?' say 'pardon'."

"But I didn't burp!" protested Bertie. He sighed. "Can I see if there's any cake?"

Gran rolled her eyes. "If you must. But don't be greedy."

Bertie pushed his way through the crowd until he spotted a waiter with a plate of cakes. There were dainty cupcakes, macaroons and lemon slices. He tugged on the waiter's sleeve, and started to fill his plate. A voice interrupted him.

"Are you having a nice time?"

Bertie turned to see a lady in a pale blue dress, with a matching hat. She was about Gran's age, but spoke terribly nicely, as if she was reading the news.

"Er, yes … yes thanks," said Bertie.

"One imagines this might not be your cup of tea," said the smiling lady.

"Oh, I don't drink tea," said Bertie. "I tried it once but I spat it out."

"I meant the garden party. Are you really having a nice time?"

"Honestly?" said Bertie, cramming a cupcake into his mouth.

"Honestly."

Bertie lowered his voice. "It's dead boring. There's nothing to do."

"Ah," said the lady. "I see."

"I mean look!" said Bertie, spraying cake crumbs everywhere. "You'd think the Queen'd do better than this. There aren't even any balloons or games! She could at least have got a bouncy castle!"

The lady seemed to find this idea amusing. "People would have to take off their hats," she said.

Bertie caught sight of Gran, who seemed to be trying to tell him something. She pointed at Bertie's companion and waved her hands as if she was swatting flies. Bertie hadn't a clue what she meant. He'd only taken four cakes so he was hardly being greedy.

Other people were waiting to meet the lady in the blue hat. She seemed surprisingly popular.

"Well, I enjoyed our little chat," she said. "Tell me, are you fond of dogs?"

"Um, yes, I've got a dog," said Bertie. "He's called Whiffer."

"I have corgis. Five. Molly, Polly, Vicky, Georgia and Jemima. Perhaps you'd like to see them?"

"Me?" said Bertie.

"Yes, my footman will show you the way."

A man in a black uniform bowed. Bertie wondered why the lady had a footman. Maybe she had bad feet? In any case, dogs were much more interesting than people. He followed the footman out of the tent to a small courtyard. A maid stood waiting with five fat little corgis, all pulling on their leads.

CHAPTER 4

Bertie let the corgis lick the cake crumbs off his hand.

"You like dogs?" asked the maid.

"Yes," replied Bertie. "Do you?"

"Can't stand 'em. Smelly, yappy things. Want to hold them for a bit?"

"Can I?"

Bertie took the leads from the maid,

who seemed glad of a break. Molly, Polly, Vicky, Georgia and Jemima sniffed round his legs.

"They haven't had their walkies yet," said the maid.

"I could take them," said Bertie. "I'm not doing anything."

The maid considered. "Okay, just round the gardens. But keep 'em on the lead."

Bertie set off. He was used to taking Whiffer for walks, but five excited corgis were a lot more trouble. They pulled in different directions and their leads got tangled under his feet. They crossed the lawn, passing the Queen's garden party. Ooops! Bertie stumbled over a tap.

WHOOSH! A garden sprinkler came on, spraying him with jets of water.

"Arghh! Oooh!" yelped Bertie,
letting go of the dog leads.

Free at last, the corgis bolted
through a flower bed and raced across
the lawn.

"NO! COME BACK!" yelled Bertie, as
they headed for the door of the big
white tent.

He chased after them. The party was
still in full flow, but as he reached the
tent he heard a terrible noise.

WOOF! CRASH! TINKLE! THUNK!

Bertie barged his way through the
crowd. He stared in horror. A waiter was
lying on the floor, surrounded by broken
cups and plates. Five fat little corgis were
clambering over him, licking up
cream and bits of cupcake.

"Crumbs!" gasped Bertie.

Dirty Bertie

The party had fallen silent. The waiter scrambled to his feet and bowed to the lady in the blue hat.

"Your Majesty, I'm most terribly sorry," he said.

Dirty Bertie

Bertie gaped. "Your *Majesty*?" Then the lady in the blue hat was the QUEEN? Why hadn't anyone warned him? He'd told her that her party was boring. He'd let her dogs loose and broken her best plates. She would probably have his head chopped off!

The Queen turned to Bertie and raised her eyebrows.

"Ah," she said. "And what do you have to say for yourself?"

Bertie gulped. He bowed low.

"Your Magicsty ... um, would you be in a photo?"

Dirty Bertie

The following Monday, Bertie's friends were waiting for him in the playground. They hadn't forgotten his ridiculous boast.

"So?" grinned Darren. "How was the party?"

"Did you see the palace?" asked Eugene.

"And did you meet her Majesty?" jeered Know-All Nick.

Bertie waited for them to stop laughing. "Actually, I did," he said. "We had a good chat."

"Liar!" snorted Nick. "You're making it up."

"Am I," said Bertie. He reached into his pocket and brought out a photo.

Dirty Bertie

Nick stared. His mouth fell open. He turned white, then green.

"You can keep it if you like," said Bertie. "I've got lots!"

CHAPTER 1

Bertie groaned.

"It's not fair! Why do I have to go?"

"It's your cousin's wedding," said Mum.

"I love weddings," sighed Suzy. "So romantic!"

"Yuck! I hate them!" said Bertie.

The last wedding his parents had dragged him to was deathly dull. He had to sit through speeches that went on for days. Even when it was time to leave there were armies of aunts waiting to kiss him. This time, his cousin Dora was marrying her fiancé, Bruce. Bertie had met drippy Dora. He couldn't see why anyone would want to talk to her – let alone marry her.

"In any case, we're going," said Mum. "Suzy's a bridesmaid and you're a pageboy."

Bertie looked horrified. *Him*? A pageboy?

"No way!" he cried.

"All you have to do is look smart," said Mum.

"I *never* look smart," said Bertie, truthfully.

"You will for Dora's wedding," said

Dirty Bertie

Mum firmly. "That's why I'm taking
you shopping on Saturday. Suzy can
find a bridesmaid's dress and we'll get
you a kilt."

"A KILT?" Bertie gasped for air.
"But that's a … a…"

"A SKIRT!"
giggled Suzy.
"HA HA!"

"Don't be silly,"
said Mum. "Bruce
is Scottish and lots
of the men will
be wearing kilts."

"But can't I just wear jeans?" begged
Bertie.

"Of course not! It's a wedding!"

Bertie groaned. This was torture!
Cruelty! It couldn't be happening!

Dirty Bertie

On Saturday morning Mum took them
to "Gladrags" wedding shop in town. The
snooty assistant helped them to choose
things to try on. Suzy picked a pretty lilac
dress with puff sleeves and went to
change. Bertie didn't choose anything.
The kilts were all too big, too baggy, too
… skirty! In the end Mum chose one for
him. Bertie took it into the changing
room and slammed the door.

A moment later, Suzy appeared.

"Oh darling, you look lovely!" said
Mum.

Suzy twirled round in front of the
mirror. She'd always dreamed of being a
bridesmaid. It was just a pity Bertie
would be there to spoil the pictures.

"Where is Bertie?" Mum frowned.
"He's been in there ages."

She knocked on the changing room
door. "BERTIE?"

"He's not here!"

"Bertie, hurry up, we're waiting!"

Dirty Bertie

"It doesn't fit. It's too big!" grumbled Bertie.

"Nonsense! Let me see!" said Mum.

"NO!"

Mum folded her arms. "Right, I'm counting to three. One, two, thr—"

BLAM! The door burst open. Bertie stomped out, scowling furiously. He was wearing a black jacket, a frilly shirt and a green kilt with a hairy sporran. It was the smallest kilt in the shop, but it practically reached Bertie's ankles.

Dirty Bertie

"It's too big!" he moaned. "I look stupid!"

"Ahh," said Suzy. "Do you want an ickle pink bow for your hair?"

"SHUT UP!" cried Bertie.

"Take no notice," said Mum. "Lots of boys wear kilts. I think you look very handsome."

Bertie scowled at his reflection in the mirror. Handsome? He couldn't go out like this! What if one of his friends saw him? It was bad enough that he had to be at Dora's wedding, but dressed in a tartan skirt? No, he wouldn't do it, not for his cousin, not for anyone. And there was nothing they could do to make him.

CHAPTER 2

Bertie climbed into the car and slumped
on the back seat. It was the morning of
Bruce and Dora's wedding. He had tried
everything to get out of wearing the
horrible hairy kilt. First he'd claimed it
was torn, then lost, then that it'd fallen
down the toilet. Mum wasn't fooled.
She said he was wearing the kilt and

he'd better get used to it.

The cars set off for the church. Bertie
was going with Suzy and Neil, the best
man. Bertie wriggled around. His kilt was
itchy. He tucked it between his legs. He
hoped it wasn't a windy day. Dad said
that Scots didn't wear anything under
their kilts – but he wasn't falling for that
one! He was wearing two pairs of pants,
just in case.

"Move over!" grumbled Suzy.

"You move over!" said Bertie.

"No! You're creasing my dress!"

Neil groaned. "Stop squabbling! You're
giving me a headache!"

Bertie rolled his eyes. What a fusspot!
If Bertie ever needed a best man it
wouldn't be Neil.

Neil looked at his watch. He checked

he had his hanky and his speech.
He checked he'd got the ring in the
little box.

"What's that?" asked Bertie.

"The wedding ring, stupid," said Suzy.

"Can I see it?"

"Certainly not!" said Neil.

"Please. Please, please, please…"

"Oh all right," groaned Neil. "Just be
careful!"

Bertie opened the box. "Wow!" he

 gasped. "Is it real gold?"

"Of course it's real!"

Bertie had never actually held

a real gold ring. The only rings he

ever got were out of Christmas crackers.
Dora must have small hands because this
ring was tiny. Bertie held it up. Maybe it
would fit him? He slipped it over his

thumb to see.

"BERTIE!" snapped Neil. "Give it back."

"Okay, okay," sighed Bertie. Some people were so impatient!

He pulled at the ring. Oops! It wouldn't come off. He tried to twist it. Argh! He tugged. He wrestled and wriggled. It wouldn't budge.

"Bertie, come ON!" groaned Neil.

"I'm … trying!" panted Bertie. "It seems to be … arrrr … stuck!"

The car turned a corner and pulled up outside the church. They all climbed out. In desperation Neil and Suzy took it in turns to try and pull the ring off Bertie's thumb.

"Keep still!"

"I am … OW! That hurts!" moaned Bertie.

It was no use. The ring was stuck like superglue. No matter how much they pulled and yanked, it wouldn't come off. A car drew up and Mum and Dad got out.

"Everything okay?" said Dad.

"It's Bertie," said Suzy. "He was playing with the ring and now he's got it stuck!"

"What?"

Bertie held up his thumb to show them.

Dirty Bertie

"It's not my fault!" he grumbled. "How was I to know it wouldn't come off?"

"Of course it's your fault," cried Neil. "You should never have touched it in the first place."

He paced up and down in a panic. This was terrible, a nightmare! Everyone was in the church waiting, and any minute now Dora would be here. But how could they start the service without a ring?

Dad checked his watch. "What are we going to do?"

Mum had an idea. "Butter!" she cried.

"What?"

"Butter – that's how you get it off! Rub his thumb with butter."

"We don't have any butter!" groaned Neil.

"What about the church hall?" said Suzy.

"Of course!" said Mum. Everyone was going to the church hall after the service for the wedding party. There would be stacks of food. They were bound to find butter somewhere.

Just then, a big white car drew up outside the church. The bride had arrived. Dora got out, trailing vast clouds of silk. Mum sprang into action.

Dirty Bertie

"Quick," she said. "I'll try to delay
them. Bertie, run to the hall with Dad."

"Me? What for?" said Bertie.

"To find some butter!" cried Mum.
"And for heaven's sake, HURRY!"

CHAPTER 3

Bertie and Dad ran to the church hall.
It was empty. The room was set out with
chairs and tables ready for the wedding
party. At the far end was a long table
with drinks and nibbles for the guests.
Bertie's eyes lit up. He hadn't eaten
anything since breakfast.

"Right," said Dad. "You look in here,

Dirty Bertie

Bertie. I'll try the kitchen."

Dad hurried off. Bertie gazed hungrily at the nibbles. He helped himself to a handful of crisps, just to help him think. What had Mum said? Oh yes, butter. Where did they keep the butter? He searched the table. Peanuts, dips, sausage rolls — but no butter.

"Find any?" shouted Dad, clattering cupboard doors in the kitchen.

"No, not yet!"

Bertie grabbed some more crisps in case the service went on a bit. Luckily his sporran was the perfect place to keep a snack. He checked to see Dad wasn't watching. Wait, what was this? Bruce and Dora's

wedding cake was sitting on a trolley.
Bertie loved cake, and this one was a
monster. It was a three cake tower
trimmed with pink roses. On the bottom
cake, written in icing, it said:

Dirty Bertie

Bertie stared. Icing – of course! Icing was just like butter. His finger hovered over the beautiful wedding cake. Should he? Time was running out and he had to get the ring off. This was his last chance. SHHLUPP! Bertie scooped up a big splodge of icing.

Mmm – not bad! He tried a pink rose. *Mmm mmm mmm.*

Remembering his mum's advice, he slathered his thumb in icing and licked it off. Whoops! The writing on the cake had got a bit smudged. Some of the letters were missing. But what about the ring? He twisted it. YES! It slid over his thumb. Genius!

"Any luck, Bertie?" cried Dad, suddenly appearing from the kitchen.

Bertie stood in front of the cake.

Dirty Bertie

"Oh … um, yes. Look, I got it off!"

He held up the ring triumphantly.

"Thank goodness!" said Dad. "You found some butter?"

"Er, sort of," said Bertie.

"Then what are we standing here for?" said Dad. "Let's get back to the church!"

Bertie glanced over his shoulder at the cake as he left. It did look a bit messy. But it was too late to do anything about it now. After all, it was only a cake. Who was going to notice?

CHAPTER 4

They reached the church and stood outside, panting for breath. Dad put his ear to the door. He groaned.

"They've already started!"

"What?" cried Bertie. "They can't have!"

"They obviously couldn't wait! We'll have to sneak in quietly," said Dad.

"But what about the ring?" said Bertie, holding it up.

"Give it to Neil! Just try not to draw attention to yourself."

Inside the church, Dora and Bruce stood at the altar. The vicar was reaching the part with the wedding vows. Neil wiped a drop of sweat from his forehead. Where in the name of heaven was Bertie? If he didn't get here soon it would be too late!

"Dora Lara Spooner," said the vicar, "do you take this man to be your husband?"

"I do," trilled Dora.

"Bruce John McDougal, do you take this woman to be your wife?"

"I do," boomed Bruce.

Dirty Bertie

Dirty Bertie

There was a long pause.

"The ring!" whispered the vicar.

"Oh, um, yes, the ring…" stammered Neil, turning bright pink. He searched his pockets as if that might help.

"Neil!" hissed Dora.

Neil shook his head helplessly. "I … er … I haven't…"

Dirty Bertie

CRASH!

Every head in the church turned round to look. Bertie had zoomed up the aisle and skidded, falling flat on his face. His kilt had flopped over, so everyone got a good view of his pants. Suzy giggled.

"BERTIE!" hissed Neil.

Dirty Bertie

Bertie got up. He pulled down his kilt and came forward. In his hand was something pink and sticky like a half-sucked sweet. He handed it over. Bruce slid the ring over Dora's finger.

"EUGH!" said Dora.

After the service they all crowded into the church hall for the wedding party. Bertie had to sit through hours of boring speeches, but he didn't care. He was off the hook. Dora grumbled that he'd almost ruined her big day, but Bruce patted his head and said no harm was done.

Neil stood up and banged on the table with a spoon.

"And now, the bride and groom will cut the cake!"

Dirty Bertie

Bertie gulped. Oh no! The cake – he'd forgotten all about it!

A lady pushed the trolley to the front where the bride and groom stood waiting. Dora took the knife ready to cut the first slice. She stared. She gasped. She looked like she might faint.

Her beautiful wedding cake – ruined! The tower was looking wonky, and there were sticky fingermarks all over it. Someone had scoffed most of the pink roses. Worst of all, the message was missing some letters, so now it read:

We rats on Your ful Day

Dirty Bertie

"EEEK! MY CAKE!" shrieked Dora.

Mum and Dad turned round. There was only one person who could have done this, and he was wearing a sticky kilt and a guilty expression.

"BERTIE!" groaned Mum.

Bertie gulped. He put his hand into his sporran.

"Um ... anyone want a crisp?"